MADE FLE

MADE FLESH

HUGH DICKINSON

YOUCAXTON PUBLICATIONS

OXFORD & SHREWSBURY

ISBN 978-1-911175-83-4
Printed and bound in Great Britain.
Published by YouCaxton Publications 2017

YouCaxton Publications
enquiries@youcaxton.co.uk

... And the Word was made flesh, and dwelt among us...
John 1: 14

FOREWORD

Although we have all been born, few of us can remember what it was like being a baby. We may have a few vignettes of early childhood and some vivid memories of adolescence and being a young adult, but those reminiscences are narrowly bounded by our own place in time and space and culture. It is from within those constraints that I have attempted to imagine what it might have been like to be a young Jew in 1st-century Galilee. The picture is inevitably contaminated by my being myself in my utterly different time and culture. It is almost impossible for me to get inside the mind of a Inuit woman in Alaska today, but the gap between me in my world and Jesus of Nazareth in his is much wider than simply temporal and cultural. He lived in a different "world". There are very few authentic hints about his life before he appeared on the banks of the Jordan and was baptised. At that point he had a transforming experience of some kind... He came back from the wilderness "full of the Spirit". What happened to him in the wilderness?

We do know what it is like for artists to give inspired performances; Janet Baker has described the experience very movingly as having something poured into her. People have described their experience of a charismatic spiritual infusion: one friend told me it was like being filled up with hot red ink; another said it was like being given a colour television for the first time after seeing only black-and-white. These experiences can be life-transforming and may last a lifetime. I have conjectured that at or after his baptism Jesus had some such an experience, one which is on the borderland of our own human experiences, and, maybe, something more. Was that "something more" different in kind or different in degree? At that point a novella gets out of its depth. Most of us paddle about in the shallows of mysticism. The saints learn how to swim out to sea. And Jesus?

§

This is not really a novella; a parable perhaps, trying to imagine what it might have been like. I have done some cursory research into places, people, flora and fauna, but there are no doubt many anachronisms or errors. My knowledge of the Essenes and Qumran is limited, but they serve a narrative purpose which doesn't depend on their historicity. The "voice" is inevitably my own and not that of a man living in those places at that time. The object of the exercise is not historical accuracy but an attempt to give flesh and blood and bone to the humanity of Jesus of Nazareth. I am not clear whether such an account has any implications for serious theologians. (Biblical quotations in the text are from the New Revised Standard Version.)

I

A soft, warm breast full of milk, tummy pains, sores, women's voices, bright lights, frightening darkness, intense pleasures, being tickled, his mother's smile, an all-enfolding love. It had been a difficult, long labour – she was only sixteen – and his right leg was twisted, so that he always walked with a slight limp, and was shorter than his brothers. He felt a burning dismay at being displaced by other babies and having to share his mother with them. His very earliest memory was resentfully watching his mother feeding a baby – his second brother probably. He had a vivid picture of this little wrinkled creature sucking noisily at her breast with its blue veins under the white skin, and Mary reaching out with her free arm and pulling him to her to kiss him, and whisper, "Another little brother for you, darling". But he was her firstborn and perhaps because of the painful birth and his limp she loved him most of all her six children. He was the oldest and even though the other boys grew taller than him he ruled the roost as the siblings grew up, running ahead of them up the hill to their uncle's sheep farm, and leading their play in the lanes and yards.

The natural world, birds, insects, flowers, trees, clouds, cornfields, the smell of new baked bread, the sweetness of first ripe figs, all ravished his senses. He would stand for half an hour transfixed with delight watching a swallow building her mud cup under the steep crag behind the village, or a yellow butterfly struggling out of its pupa under a leaf. He would creep out on a hot summer night and lie on his back in the meadow looking up at the stars. He had a sense of being attended to by the villages up in the sky looking down on him. People said if you looked carefully you could see great beasts marching across the night: the Goat, the Lion, the Bull. Some said the stars talked to you if you listened.

Once when he was about four years old he was lying on his tummy out in the meadow on a spring morning, watching a small black-and-white spider picking its way between the flower stems, when all of a sudden the whole world went still. The spider stopped moving; the lark stopped singing; there was no wind; the buttercup flowers above his head turned to motionless solid gold; the women stopped chattering in the house; the grass stems were made of jewelled emerald, and the whole valley was immersed in a huge suffocating Presence, so vast that it was almost impossible to breathe. The landscape and every single thing in it, every leaf and twig and insect, was enfolded in a glowing radiance. There was a timeless moment of piercing joy. For one long ecstatic instant he felt himself to be part of everything and everything was part of him. He was being held. Then there was a burst of laughter from the window and the world started up again. The spider struggled on its way, the lark sang, the breeze moved the flowers and he could breathe freely. But that moment of ecstasy was etched on his memory for the rest of his life. He was to have the same experience from time to time in later years but never with quite the same diamond clarity and intensity. It always came unannounced and left inexplicably. But he knew from that moment that everything is, all the time and always, enfolded in an invisible glory.

In the spring he went up to his uncle's sheep farm to watch the lambs being born and was at once recruited to help a ewe which was in trouble giving birth. His small neat hand could feel around inside the bleating animal to find the lamb's displaced leg and haul the slippery little creature out. He wondered if the midwife had done that for him. He loved going up to the farm, and made friends with the chickens and their chicks and played with the farm cat's kittens. Sometimes he slept with the other boys up in the fold under the stars on a smelly fleece in a shelter of branches. He tried to help with the milking but his hands were too small to squeeze the goats' teats, but he enjoyed helping his cousins to sort the animals out. His uncle told him, "Look at their tails, lad, goats stick their tails up, sheep let 'em hang down. Sheep on this side of the hurdles and goats on the far side." It was amazing to watch them all obediently crowding in after his uncle in the evening when they came into the fold for the night. One lamb was rejected by its mother, and he was allowed to carry it home to see if he could save its life. Mary gave him a jar with a spout to feed it on goats' milk. It sucked his finger and seemed to be flourishing, but one morning he came out to the shed to find it cold and as stiff as a board. He was heartbroken.

In winter he would join his father in the carpenter's shop watching the muscles ripple under his dark skin as he sawed up planks and beams or chipped away at them with an adze. The wood chips flew all over the floor, smelling of pine resin and fresh sap. Once he cut the palm of his hand on a chisel and howled with pain and shock at the flow of blood. Joseph picked him up and sat him on the workbench and went into a dark corner to come back with a handful of spider's webs which he wrapped round the cut and tied in with an old rag. "Don't go playing with sharp tools lad. You'll end up getting hurt." The wound healed in ten days, but the scar stayed with him. He adored his father, the long grey beard and dark twinkling eyes – and always the smile. Joseph made a leather sling for him and showed him how to whizz it round and let go of one strap so the stone flew off much further than he could throw it. Joseph put an old pot up on a wall and after three attempts knocked it over with a satisfying crack of broken shards. "Useful for keeping lions away", he said with a grin.

For the boy Jesus, Joseph was the perfect father. He taught him the carpenter's trade, the different woods, how to use and sharpen tools and carve tenons and mortices. He taught him the names of the local flowers and common birds. In spring and autumn, flocks of strange birds came flooding through Galilee, fleeing the snow and frost of the northern sea for the warmth of Egypt in the autumn or making the return journey to escape the baking desert heat in the spring. Some of them were regular visitors like the swallows, hoopoes, orioles and purring turtle doves; others unfamiliar wanderers, occasionally eagles high overhead, kites and buzzards passing to and fro. By mid summer the wide drifts of crocuses, anemones and yellow daisies in the fields had all dried up, but their reawakening was always a joyous first sign of spring. The summers were hot and dry and the streams where the women went every day to fetch water and wash the clothes sometimes became no more than trickles. In those times of drought, water was a precious gift for which the Holy One was always blessed. There was a "well" below the village but it was just a clay-lined hollow fed by run-off from the hillside; in dry weather the water became green and sour and full of frogs. Some of the larger houses had courtyards with deep cisterns fed by gutters from the tiled roofs. But for most village women it meant a tiring slog down to the well and a half-full pitcher of rank water to carry back on an aching shoulder.

One summer a team of well diggers visited the village. There was a lot of noisy bargaining with the village elders, but eventually a deal was done. First they had to spend time locating the underground spring, and then they had to dig down to find it; if they didn't find water they wouldn't charge for the digging. The wife of the head of the team, who all seemed to be siblings or cousins, was an enormously fat black woman with dark eyes in a lined face wrinkled like an old fig. The morning after they arrived the lad followed them out onto the hillside. Most of the men sat in the shade watching the woman walking slowly along the hill with her husband. They came to a slight dip, when she nodded and the man handed her a couple of short willow sticks. Very slowly she walked to and fro from side to side of the hollow, holding a stick in each hand. From time to time she would nod to the man and he would put a stone down. She spent most of the morning like that walking slowly back and forth. Then they all gathered in the shade for a midday meal and a rest. The woman beckoned the lad over and gave him some olives and a bit of bread and asked him his name. "Well, young Jesus Josephson, tomorrow you may see a miracle – or perhaps the third day." When she smiled her eyes almost vanished in the crinkles.

Early the next morning they brought their team of mules up the hillside with all their tools and belongings and began to dig. They worked in groups of four, taking turns to dig and to remove the spoil and then to rest. The following morning a gang of local men from the village joined the well diggers, helping to carry the rubble away and to construct a steep winding path down into the hole they had excavated. That evening one of the men wielding a bronze crowbar at the bottom gave a shout and came up with a jar of soil which was dark with moisture. Everyone cheered.

The next morning Josephson crept out before anyone was stirring, scrambled up the hill, and looked over the edge of the hole. The bottom of the well was full of crystal clear water. The well digger's wife silently joined the boy as the sun rose and said to him, "Well, lad, there's your miracle."

He never forgot that moment of piercing astonishment. Rabbi Reuben said everyone should sing a psalm of praise to the Lord, "For His mercy is for ever and ever," just as they did when the first spring rains came, and the flowers suddenly reappeared.

When he was twelve his father started taking him to the synagogue. Rabbi Reuben spotted the boy's intelligence and the rapt attention with which he listened to the scripture readings. He taught him to read, first Aramaic then a bit of Hebrew. He then found the lad turning up on his doorstep asking him about the readings he had heard. He was fascinated by the stories of the Garden of Eden and the patriarchs in *Genesis* and *Exodus*. He loved the psalms and learned some of them by heart. He started to think. Often his first words when he arrived were, "Rabbi, I've been thinking......" and he would look at Reuben with that intense searching gaze. Reuben was a great one for stories. He told the boy some of the sayings of the fathers, particularly the funny ones; he made up stories himself about the animals round the farms. Once the lad asked him, "Is that true?" "What do you think?" The boy frowned. "No, I don't think so. But perhaps it's true in a sort of sideways way?" Sometimes the questions he came up with baffled the old man. "Why did God rebuke Job even though he was right?" "Why didn't God allow Moses to go into the Promised Land?" "Why did God make the serpent?" "I know God is present, but why is He so absent?" The old man was startled. He looked at him and nodded. "Yes. The absence of the Lord's Presence is less terrifying than the presence of his Absence, isn't it?" When the boy left the Rabbi watched him limping up the lane and shook his head.

At Passover one year after the bar-mitsvah the carpenter Joseph turned up on Rabbi Reuben's doorstep. He was a bit hesitant but the old man told him to come and sit down. "You want to talk about young Jesus, is that it?", he asked. "Well, yes. We can't make him out. Always asking questions. Acting a bit strange. Burst into tears when we killed the lamb, kept stroking its fleece, although I told him it's what the Lord has commanded. He was horrified when I told him how many were killed in the Temple at Passover. He spends a lot of time out in the fields and up the hill, all on his own watching the birds or looking at the stars. He's a good lad, no real trouble, willing to help and learning the trade, but always questions, questions, questions. Yes, truth to tell, some questions I've secretly asked myself but never spoken out loud. Sometimes I don't know what to say. And he's got bits of the Torah by heart. When I can't provide an answer he just stands and looks at me. It's a bit unnerving. Do you think he's got a bad spirit?"

The old man stroked his beard. "Yes, questions, always good questions. But no, not a bad spirit. When he reads the Prophets he's always listening to them as if they were here shouting outside in the street. He asked me last week, "Why did the Kings and Priests not listen to what the Prophets were saying? Why did they kill them?" And then, "Is it like that nowadays in Jerusalem? Are they still not listening?" I told him we're still in exile, as long as the Romans are here. But then he went on, "Yes I know that's what you keep saying, that we're still in exile and that there are no more prophets to put us right. But we've got the Scriptures. Can't they *read*? Don't they *listen*?" The old man shrugged and smiled at Joseph. "Then he looked straight at me and asked me, "You read the Scriptures, Rabbi. You taught me to read, and I bless God for that. I don't think you taught me how to *listen*. But I try to listen. Sometimes they speak." Reuben paused and looked up at the hill behind the house. "No, not a bad spirit, Joseph. I don't think he will ever tell a lie. Perhaps something more troubling. I will teach him what I know, but I think there's a hunger in him. Yes, a hunger. A hunger for God, Blessed be He. Tell him, if he comes here with his questions I will always make him welcome."

One day, months later, when young Josephson went to call on the Rabbi, he found a stranger, a younger man, sitting deep in conversation with him under the fig tree in the garden. He apologised and was about to back out when the Rabbi called him over. "Come in lad, come in and meet my friend Nathanael. He's on his way down to the Salt Sea. He'll answer some of your questions I'm sure. A real scholar." The stranger was a tall, gaunt young man with a dark complexion, a neatly trimmed black beard, dressed in a spotless white shirt and sandals. He greeted Jesus warmly. "Come over here, boy, and let me have a look at you. So this is your young prophet, Reuben, is it? Sit down boy, sit down, and let's have some conversation. So: always asking questions, eh?" That afternoon was one Jesus never forgot. He went home seething with excitement. At last someone who seemed to speak out of a deep well of knowledge and wisdom. Not just quoting other teachers. He belonged to one of the prophetic communities down by the Salt Sea, and as he rose to leave he had turned to the lad and said, "If ever you want to go on with our conversation, young man, come down and visit us one day. You'll be very welcome."

When old Rabbi Reuben died the following year, the boy wept for him for days. After the harvest was gathered in he asked Joseph to give him leave to go and spend some time with the Rabbi's friend Nathanael in one of the religious communities at Qumran, down by the Salt Sea. "Abba, I feel God, Blessed be He, is calling me to find a new teacher." Joseph refused at first; who would help him with the work? But Jesus persisted. He pointed out that he had four younger brothers, James, Joseph, Judas and Simon, all of whom could beat him at wrestling three times out of four. Eventually, with a heavy heart Joseph watched his eldest son walking away into the sunrise. He never saw him again.

II

It took Jesus six days to walk up past Jerusalem and then on down into the sultry heat of the valley of the Salt Sea. On this side there was the large settlement of Qumran, and beyond it a scatter of small hamlets with other Community enclosures, courtyards surrounded by cells behind high walls, ploughed fields and tidy meadows with sheep and cattle, vineyards and groves of figs and sycamores. He had to ask at several doors before he found the community where Nathanael lived. He was welcomed in at the gate by a large bald man, also with a neatly trimmed beard and in a spotless white shirt, who sat him down on a bench by the gate and brought him a cup of water. "I expect you're parched, my son, aren't you?" Then to the boy's acute embarrassment he knelt down, pulled a basin out from under the bench and proceeded to wash his feet. "Nasty blister there, lad. I'll get you some ointment. Now, let's go and find Nathanael." That first smiling welcome turned out to be true of everyone the lad met in his new home, for after a couple of weeks he began to think of the community as his spiritual home.

At first he was completely lost. He found himself placed in a group of a dozen young probationers, sleeping, working and eating together. To begin with they teased him for his Northern brogue, but he was a quick learner and gradually adapted to their Judean accent. The routine was strict: prayers, labouring in the farm, reading scriptures, teaching and discipline sessions, lectures, daily ablutions, washing clothes, preparing vegetables – some of the brothers refused to eat meat – so every moment of the day was designated for some task or duty. Sabbaths were particularly strict, with many more rules and regulations than old Rabbi Reuben had taught him. Occasionally the whole community would walk over to Qumran to hear the Teacher of Righteousness preach, sometimes for three or four hours at a time. He was heard in rapt silence by the men who gathered around him hanging on his every word. The young Josephson was totally absorbed. What must it be like to have such power over men's hearts? The force of the Teacher's voice was hypnotic, although his teachings were often hotly debated afterwards among the Elders, many of whom were from priestly or Pharisee families. The monasteries were always seething with discussions and disputes. As he listened to them the young Josephson would sometimes feel a sudden "YES!" to something he heard or read, as if it struck a responding chord in his heart. Sometimes he listened uneasily as if in his guts he knew that something was wrong, even if he couldn't say what it was.

This austere life was rendered much more agreeable by the ethos of kindness and care which permeated the whole community, although sometimes, when the debates got rather heated, intense passions came to the surface. Life was made easier for the latest probationer when they discovered that he was a competent carpenter, so instead of sweating under the sun in the fields he was put to work making furniture or helping to roof in the new cells which were being built all over the settlement to accommodate a steady stream of new members. He was also singled out by Nathanael for special classes, because he could not only read and write but already knew some of the Scriptures by heart, and could always be relied on to ask interesting questions.

In the autumn he was given permission to go home for a couple of weeks to catch up with family news. The news was heartbreaking. Joseph had died after falling off a roof and the family was in deep mourning. His mother wept on his shoulder, sobbing, "If only you had been here, son, it wouldn't have happened!" He held her tight and sobbed with her, "Oh Abba! Oh Abba! If only I had been here for you. But the Lord, Blessed be He, gives and takes away". His brothers looked at him with puzzled frowns, not knowing what to make of him, but he quickly slipped back into his rural speech. James had turned into a tough young man and had arranged for his sister Miriam to be married to the son of the local builder. The business seemed to be thriving and there was no problem about her dowry. Although his mother begged him to stay he now really had no role at home. It was a sad visit but he felt oddly light-hearted on the way back as he reached the crest of the hill above the Salt Sea and could look down on what he now felt was home. Here his hunger for God was being fed.

What he learned over the next five years was just how deeply the social and religious divisions in Israel penetrated into every corner of the land and affected even the most everyday activities. The Community believed that they were themselves the faithful Remnant of Israel prophesied in the Scriptures; that the End Time of the Messiah was at hand; that He would inaugurate the Restoration of Israel, purify the Promised Land, expel the Romans and all Gentile pollutions and establish a new Davidic Kingdom. But then there were more disputes: would Messiah be in the line of David or of Aaron or of Melchisadek? Would he be a warrior or a priest or prophet like the Teacher? Scripture was silent on so many urgent issues. Was Herod's vast Temple idolatrous, as some brothers insisted? The Temple authorities were notoriously corrupt. Some in the Community said it was haunted by demons. Josephson was shocked. It was the Temple of God, and held the Holy of Holies! Demons in God's House!

There were so many arguments. Surely armed insurrection was permissible? Was there life after death? Should Jews use Roman coinage, which surely must be unclean with the Emperor's head on it.? Was the Covenant vocation of Israel for Israel alone or for all the nations? How much authority did the Traditions of the Elders have? Were all their detailed purity and Sabbath rules as authoritative as the Torah? How did they deal with possession by demons? With leprosy? With menstrual blood? With dead bodies? With divorce? Every question and every answer had advocates and opponents. The arguments went on at meals, in the fields, in classrooms, in the dormitories. They had been going on for many decades. Nathanael commented wryly, "If one Jew keeps the whole law for one day the Kingdom of God will come!"

In some communities there were teams of healers and exorcists, and the peasant folk used to come down with sick and injured and demented friends or children to ask for help. Nathanael was an Elder in the group of healers and Jesus Josephson found himself drawn to get involved with the crowds of poor folk and deeply moved by their suffering. He watched miserably as children died in their fathers' arms. He could do nothing to help. Back in Nazareth he had sometimes found that by gently stroking a donkey's or sheep's swollen leg for half an hour he could ease the pain and reduce the swelling. When he told Nathanael this the Elder took his hands and looked closely at his palms. "Did your hands feel warm when you did that?" "Yes, quite hot sometimes, and a sort of tingling up my spine". "Ah, yes. I think you have a gift, my lad. The Lord gives some people special gifts. When you do that, always say a blessing. And you should use the gift. It's like using a saw. The more you use it the more it comes."

So he began to use his gift. But it was tiring. All the endless noisy arguments, the crowds and the crying children he found exhausting. He was never alone. He longed to be back in the hills of Galilee with nothing but the larks and sorrowful doves and the endless sky; or even better, at night under the stars and no sound at all except the distant barking of a dog, and the brooding Presence of God's Spirit enfolding everything. The God who had promised Abraham that his descendents would be as many as those stars up there in the night sky. He ached for silence under those huge constellations. One day Nathanael asked him if all was well. "You look tired, lad. Ah, yes, silence. Not much of it here, is there? I go up into the hills sometimes, just to get a drink of the Spirit. Would you like to come with me one day?"

They crossed the Jordan at the ford as it was getting light one morning, and then climbed steeply up for an hour among the craggy cliffs. Josephson's lame leg was aching when Nathanael stopped in the shade of a great over-hanging rock, out of the intense glare of the sun. Just behind it there was an entrance to a cave. "Always have a good sniff before you settle down. Leopards like to lie up in these caves. A juicy probationer on the doorstep would be a gift from God – well, for the leopard if not for the probationer." They said a psalm together and then Nathanial said, "You've got a skin of water? Good. Enjoy God's silence. I'll pick you up at dusk. We'll need some light to find the path down". He spent the morning simply opening his heart to what Nathaniel had called "God's silence". At noon he had a gulp of water and then lay down and fell asleep.

The sun was setting when Nathaniel shook him awake. He stumbled to his feet and started to apologise. "Don't worry lad. Sleep is a gift from God. He knows you need it. He gives his beloved sleep. So just bless his Name." After that, regularly once a week, the two of them went up to the cave and the overhanging rock to drink in the silence of the Spirit. When Nathanael was away or busy Josephson would go up on his own. Then he got permission to leave the previous evening and spend the night either under the stars or in the cave. He always built a small fire in the entrance to deter wild beasts He felt his hunger for God was being much more richly fed up in the silence of the crags than by all the busy chatter in the community. The solitude was drenched in the Spirit.

One night he had to retreat into the cave when a thunder storm came rumbling down the valley. The monstrous crashes of thunder and the shafts of lightning were almost continuous, echoing and rebounding off the cliffs and dislodging stones which came clattering down all round him. He stood out in the entrance to the cave as the downpour swept past on a sudden wind, relishing the torrent soaking his clothes with delicious coolness after the sultry heat of the day. Suddenly the words of a psalm came into his head and he sang aloud the ancient verses of praise to the Voice of the Lord:

The Voice of the Lord splits the flames of fire,
the Voice of the Lord shakes the wilderness;
the Voice of the Lord shakes the wilderness of Kadesh.
The voice of the Lord makes the oak trees writhe
and strips the forest bare.
In the Temple of the Lord all are crying "Glory!"

Long after the storm had rumbled away into the Negev he stood there in a rapture of joy. Then something changed. The utter silence of the night ceased to be the absence of noise. It became an enfolding Presence. He knelt and fell on his face pulling his damp cloak over his head, not daring to move, hardly daring to breathe. He lay there until the sky lightened and dawn slid over a land refreshed by rain.

III

The following years were turbulent times for the communities in the Jordan Valley. The authorities in Jerusalem became more active in challenging them. Some of their leaders were detained and taken to Jerusalem for questioning. The intensity of the factional disputes occasionally became violent. Crowds of Zealots gathered in the towns, and then up in the hills, and the Roman legionaries were much more visible in the streets and markets of the towns and villages, always on the alert for trouble. Josephson wandered from one community to another, listening to the preachers and teachers, studying the Scriptures and the ancient papyrus scrolls. Everyone was talking about an End Time, a new Messianic Age, and wondering when the Restoration of Israel would come. Was violent revolt the only way? What about the Maccabean martyrs? They fought and won. Some of his friends said violence could never produce peace. Others said there must be God's retribution on sinners. He decided not to take the vow of Community membership after his three years' probation – there were just too many different opinions and teachings to be able to vow to observe and defend them. He was always welcomed warmly when he came back; his skills and his healing gifts were highly valued. He listened, asked questions, watched and kept his own counsel.

Twice a year he travelled back to Nazareth, delighting in the growing families of his brothers and sisters. James and his children were now living in his mother's house, and although they welcomed him with open arms there was always a sense of constraint. As first-born he was head of the family, but he was still unmarried and it looked as if James was now actively filling that role and talked of his lively boys inheriting the land and the business. His mother, still a handsome and active middle aged woman, would ask him if he had found a wife yet, or could she ask one of their neighbours for a girl, but he would only smile and kiss her and say he had a vocation now. Did she understand? She had a kind of inner serenity; perhaps she did. In his third year as a probationer he'd had a long discussion with Nathanael about marriage. Some of the communities allowed members to have wives and families in the local villages, but all the men in Nathanael's community were celibate. Nathanael insisted that if the Faithful Remnant of Israel was to be ready for the imminent End Time they must be like warriors preparing for a battle. Women and children were a distraction. Like the Prophets Elijah and Elisha, when the Time came they would be fully engaged in the contest for the Restoration of Israel. Women were a temptation. Remember Eve. Young Jesus Josephson was puzzled. He thought of his mother and his sisters. His youngest sibling Rachel was a handsome girl. He watched her as she hung out the washing to dry. Some local lad was going to be lucky. He noticed how she was maturing into a woman, her arms and bosom filling out, her smile and side glances more consciously enticing. Part of him longed to have a girl like Rachel by his side, in his bed, in his arms, satisfying his need, bearing his sons. He loved the way James' oldest boy, Joseph, ran to his father and clasped his legs. He longed to have a young Joseph on his own knees, to be to him what his father had been to him.

As he stood in what was now James' workshop the smell of cedar wood and animal glue brought back vivid memories of running up to his own father, just here, beside this work bench. He stroked the smooth grain of a newly planed plank and thought of fathers and sons. Fathers and sons. Father Abraham and the lad Isaac. What must the old man have felt, taking his puzzled son up that mountain, knowing what he had to do? His only precious son, born in his extreme old age. What kind of God would ask any father to kill his own son? A test? Did he have to prove that he really believed that this miraculous child could still be replaced by another miracle to validate God's promise of thousands of descendants? But a second son would not be his uniquely precious darling Isaac. Nothing could replace him, not even descendants as many as the stars of heaven. What kind of God *is* He?

He thought of King David howling with grief in the little room above the gateway when he heard the news that his treacherous son Absolom had died a humiliating death. "O Absolom! My son! My son! Would to God I had died for you, O Absolom, my son, my son!" Is that what Israel's God felt about his faithless people? A heart-break like that? He thought about King David seeing Bathsheba bathing on the roof of the house just below the palace windows. Had she looked up to him in the open casement and smiled? He had himself once come across three girls bathing in a pool just below a waterfall in a wooded mountain stream. He stood and watched them with the blood pounding in his throat. They caught sight of him and screamed, running for their clothes and away into the trees. The memory of rounded limbs and breasts and wet hair haunted him for weeks. He smiled ruefully. If he had been married that lustful glance would have been a kind of betrayal of his wife, a sort of mental adultery. He thought about the Song of Solomon. He had dozens of wives and concubines. He thought about the Prophet Hosea's heartbreak when he discovered the unfaithfulness of his darling young wife. Not once or twice, but time after time. And always, at God's command, he took her back, not only into his house but into his bed. Polluted goods, which surely polluted him too. What *sort* of God was that? A God who went on loving his faithless people without any conditions, whatever they did? That surely couldn't be right. Could it? He was a Holy God and his holiness a consuming fire. Questions, but no answers

These were the questions and many others which he would ask the enfolding silence as he stood out at night on some hillside under the stars. His wanderings round Judah took him through Jericho and Jerusalem. Jerusalem stunned and exhausted him and Herod's vast Temple troubled him. He was shocked by the money-changers fleecing the pilgrims up from the countryside, by the way the priests and scribes flaunted their rich clothing. He watched as pilgrims had their own farm animals rejected for some small blemish and being forced to buy one from a Temple trader. He watched as one in the line of half a dozen priests tied up the animal's legs, pulled it head back and slit its throat, and hung it up by its back legs, still twitching, on a hook to let the blood drain into a bowl below it. The man was bald and grossly fat, his apron and arms stained with blood and crawling with flies. He took a swig from a jar of wine. When he saw Josephson watching him he grinned drunkenly and nodded at the bowl. "God's wine, that is." Were there demons even here in the Temple? He looked up and saw that swallows were building their nests under the cornices of the great building. God obviously welcomed them. Did he not mind about a drunken priest?

Josephson was even more dismayed by the crowds of desperately poor people begging in the streets. Outside the Temple precinct there were blind men and lame men propped up against the walls and serving as suitable recipients for the obligatory daily donations to the poor from pious worshippers coming and going into the Temple. There were raddled prostitutes lurking under the arches and hiding from the Temple police who would drive them away with blows. He stumbled over one girl with a bruised face crouched in a doorway, no older than his sister Rachel, trying to suckle a baby girl crying in her arms. He stopped to help her up, put his cloak over her to cover her nakedness and gave her a bit of bread and some cheese. He asked her name "It's Mary, sir, " she sobbed. She told him she had just been thrown out by her husband who had beaten her for producing a girl and not a boy. He felt a seething rage rising in his throat. Suddenly he understood why the prophet had heard God saying "I hate divorce!" This was sheer cruelty. It was worse. It was demonic. And yet it was here that God had been faithfully worshipped by daily sacrifices for a thousand years – the heartbeat of Israel, the Holy of Holies, and a weeping woman.

People were beginning to stop and look at them. All he could do was to give her his cloak and a blessing for her baby. The sooner he was out of these seething streets the better. He could see why the communities of the Remnant of

Israel down by the Salt Sea said that Jerusalem had become a place of corruption and idolatry. Was Herod's huge temple itself just another Golden Bull? What about "the widow, the orphan and the stranger in your land"? It wasn't just the ignorant folk who were sinners. Israel herself was living in sin. He stood aside in a passage way to let a contingent of soldiers tramp past. And then all of a sudden it happened again. The world went still. Everyone was motionless. There was total silence. A flock of pigeons hung motionless in the sky. A woman in an upper window beating a carpet stood stock still, her carpet curved unmoving in the air. Everything was enfolded in radiance, the whole street, the birds, the cobble stones, the woman in the window, the soldiers in their armour, everything was glowing. The now familiar piercing ecstasy engulfed him, although this time at the centre of the glory he sensed an aching sadness, beauty seen through tears. An eternal moment of joy and a grief outside time. The Presence was here. Then it was gone. The busy city went on its raucous way, the soldiers marched on, and his cheeks were wet. A passing old woman looked at him, smiled sympathetically.

Wandering back down into Galilee he found some work in the fishing villages on the shores of the Galilee Sea, mending broken oars and repairing leaking boats. One boat was pulled up on the beach upside down while four young men argued what to do what to do about a badly splintered plank. Apparently they had hit a rock in the darkness the previous night, and now their trade was at risk. He put down his bag of tools and went to look at the damage. They stood up and glared at him suspiciously until he said he thought he could mend it if they could find some timber. When he showed them his tools the largest of them, a huge young man with muscles like an ox asked him, "What you going to charge, mister?" "Just a mug of water, a bit of bread and somewhere to lay my head under cover." The big man nodded to one of the others. "Go and ask mother if we can bring this carpenter in tonight. He won't get it done this afternoon. We've got to find some planks. Looks like another storm coming up. Not a night to sleep out, I reckon."

Josephson found the fisherman's thick dialect hard to follow, but when it began to rain they led him through a narrow street and into a flat roofed house with some oars propped up by the door and a pile of nets in the narrow courtyard. The man's mother was in mourning – her husband had been drowned during a winter storm – but she welcomed Josephson warmly, gestured for him to sit down with the other men, put mugs of rough wine in front of them and then a fish stew with hunks of coarse bread to mop up the juices. He thanked her warmly for her hospitality as she bustled round serving them. She smiled at him and patted his back. Some other women peered in through the open doorway to look at this stranger with his neatly trimmed beard. He slept that night on a comfortable straw mattress in the little guest room built onto the end of the house over the shed where the animals were penned. It was smelly but warm and dry.

News of his trade skills spread along the shore. He spent several weeks mending boats and furniture down there by the lake, and Peter's mother made it clear that she was happy to have him in her guest room. Perhaps she thought he might take a fancy to one of her girls. He got to know and admire Peter and Andrew, and further up the shore helped their neighbours James and John, the family of Zebedee who had been Peter's father's partner. On a couple of nights Josephson went out with them on the lake and was impressed by the skill and strength they needed to manage the heavy boats and their cumbersome nets. Even young John was deft with the ropes although he was only just getting a downy fuzz on his chin. They joked that they had all been born in their boats. One night they had no luck until Josephson spotted a ruffling of the surface in the path of the moon, They pulled the boat round and hauled in two nets full of leaping fish, and sold most them early the next morning when the village women came down to bargain and buy fresh food for the day. One of them smiled at him and said he had brought them good luck. Was he going to settle down there?

If the weather was bad they would sit round the fire and listen to him telling them his dreams of the Restoration of Israel and the beginning of the Messianic Age. John asked him if there would be fishing in the New Age. He smiled at the boy and put his arm round his shoulders. "I'm sure there will." John was a dreamy, imaginative youth with curly hair and a ready smile. He was fascinated by Josephson's tales of Jerusalem and the Salt Lake communities, and even more by the stories from the Torah and the promises of the Restoration of Israel which the Teacher of Righteousness preached. Josephson began to teach him how to read and write and a bond of affectionate friendship grew between them. Josephson sometimes looked at the boy and wondered, maybe this is what his son would have been like if he had had one.

IV

In spite of these new friendships he found the noise and chatter of the Lake villages was hard to escape. No one was ever alone. His hunger for the enfolding silence increased every day. When the first almond blossom was coming into full flower all up the slopes above the Lake he left his new friends, promising them that he would be back one day, and set out on the rough road to the north where Hermon loomed mistily on the horizon with patches of snow on its upper slopes. The mountain seemed to be calling to his soul. It was a long three days' walk and then a steep climb. Shepherds on the hills cheerfully gave him ewes' milk and goats' cheese in exchange for a bit of human conversation and news of the great world down there. He told them of the rumours of the End Time and speculation about Messiah. Some of them didn't even know what the word meant. He slept with them under a rough shelter among the animals inside a semicircular sheepfold made out of thorn branches against the foot of a low cliff to keep predators out. He attended to animals that were lame or injured. Just outside the sheep fold there was a little niche in the cliff. He noticed a shrine with a crude female clay figure with wide hips and big breasts; below it was a sheep's skull with some wild flowers stuck into it. Astarte, one of the old heathen gods of the land from ancient times, he thought, and shuddered. When would Israel be purified?

He asked the shepherd if he could look in on his way down next day. The old man grinned knowingly, "Ah, going up to ask the Green Lady for a favour, then? Want a son, eh? The altar's just above the oak wood. Just follow the path. Can't miss it. On the right." He accepted a hunk of rye bread, a bit of goat's cheese and some honey comb wrapped in a dock leaf, and set off climbing as the sun rose. The path seemed to be well worn, and he felt a pang of anxiety. Who might he meet? The flowers up here were unfamiliar, but a small flock of hoopoes flickered among the oak trees, heading north, and he heard an oriole calling. Just before noon he climbed out of the woods onto a closely nibbled grass slope sprinkled with small flowers, and in half of an hour reached the nearest summit. The main mountain ridge went on in a series of higher tops towards the north. Although the wind was warm from the southern deserts, it was cold up here; there were still patches of snow in the gullies. He scooped up an icy handful to quench his thirst and turned to look back down the mountainside.

So this was the Promised Land, flowing with milk and honey. It was heart-achingly beautiful. He found tears of joy running down his cheeks. Far out to the West there was a streak of silver on the horizon – the edge of the Great Sea. To the south a glitter of Galilee Lake and, away beyond, the hills of Judea blue in the spring haze. This beautiful gift of God promised to Abraham and his descendants, richly clothed in orchards, corn fields, streams and lush pasture lands. To the North there was Lebanon with its cedar forests, and beyond that, so people said, the great mountains of Anatolia and Greece. And, somewhere beyond that, mighty Rome with its terrifying armies. He looked down the slope in front to him, awash with the mauve of crocuses and tiny irises. Surely the Emperor in Rome never wore purple robes as fine as this. There was a great brooding Presence all over the land. Was it also brooding over the corrupt and idolatrous people in Galilee and over the Gentile troops tramping across it like herds of pigs? A surge of anger tightened his throat.

Looking down, his eye fell on a rectangular slab of limestone on a level area above the trees. An altar to the ancient goddess of the High Places, Astarte the Green Lady, the shepherd had called her. The sudden burning rage was almost choking him. The prophets had told them, generation after generation, to destroy these high places. Here on this beautiful slope the old demons still clung on and seduced men's hearts. And down there in the haze the Roman legions were stamping on the Promised Land in their heavy boots, while away in distant Jerusalem Herod's Temple and the Priests were sucking the life out of the souls of God's people, neglecting "the orphans and widows and strangers in the land" and exploiting the poor. It wasn't just Astarte. The whole land, God's beautiful land, was full of demons. The land was sick, that's what the prophet had said, the fields are sick. Would the Restoration of Israel for which his friends down in the Salt Sea communities prayed every day – would it ever come? Would God relent one day and bring his people out of this spiritual Babylon and reign among us in this sick land and heal it? What will he do about all our sins? If it was to be a holy war, how many peasants, their women and children would lose their lives? Sheep without a shepherd.

Sick at heart he set off down the hill. As he passed the ancient altar slab he saw it was stained with blood with flies crawling on it. Baalzebub, Lord of Flies! People were still coming up to this high place to worship the ancient demons. On his way down through the oak woods he stepped aside from the well worn path to relieve himself behind a tree and watched a group of chattering women go by, carrying baskets of fruit and bunches of flowers. They didn't see him, but he felt a surge of anger at them, but then pity for them too, innocent laughing women, like a little flock of sheep straying into wolf country. He went on down past his friendly shepherd's shelter, begged a drink of milk and some nuts and slept in a hamlet in the marshy fields at the foot of the mountain. There were a lot of sick folk lying around so he slept in the sultry open air under a leaning rock. In the morning he found his face and arms were covered in insect bites which itched for days.

He crossed the Jordan to the East bank to steer clear of hostile Samaritans and took the rough track down the river. That night he found himself shivering even though it was very warm. By the time he re-crossed the river below Bethany he had a high fever and could hardly stagger up the hill to the little hospice on the edge of the village, built by members of the Community as a refuge for travellers going up to Jerusalem for the festivals. The brother at the gate recognized him and half carried him in to a cell where he collapsed onto the pallet shivering convulsively. He remembered very little of the following days – just a blur of hushed voices, of someone wiping the sweat off his face with a cold cloth, holding a mug of water to his lips and covering him with a sheep's fleece when he threw it off, all mixed up with strange hallucinations, terrifying nightmares of men with the heads of animals pursuing him, and crowds of women among the trees laughing derisively at him, and a little boy bleeding on an ancient altar stone while a hooded figure in black with a bloody knife loomed over him. It was more horrific because the stone slab was covered with fresh flowers which turned into flies. In his terror he cried out, "Abba! Oh Abba! Help me! Help me!" In the darkness it seemed that he was suddenly enfolded in Joseph's arms as he had often been as a child. Sobbing with relief he turned over again and fell into a dreamless sleep.

When the fever left him he was as weak as a new born lamb. One of the hospice brothers looked after him as tenderly as a woman, fed him gruel and lentil broth. One day he woke from an afternoon sleep to find a young man sitting beside his bed reading a scroll. "Ah, good. You're awake, my friend. Peace be with you. My name's Lazarus and they tell me you're Jesus Josephson from Nazareth. I supply the brothers here with herbs and vegetables from our garden. My sisters grow them and I bring them up on the donkey. They tell me you're a great reader, and might like some company. I'm just reading this scroll of the Prophet Daniel. I don't know what to make of him. They said you might know what it's all about. This vision of the Son of Man coming to restore Israel after the Gentile empires. What's that about? The brothers are saying it will be soon. Some pilgrims going up to the Temple said they'd heard there's a new prophet preaching the New Age down by the Jordan".

Josephson sat up and smiled at the young man, took the scroll and began to read it aloud. It was all strange visionary stuff. But his young visitor was obviously keenly intelligent, so the next hour passed in friendly conversation. It was only when he got up and turned away to leave that Josephson saw that the further side of Lazarus's face was disfigured by a large purple blotch. Lazarus must have seen his startled expression, for he turned back and put his hand up to his face. "I'm, sorry, yes, I've had it since I was born. The priests say it isn't leprosy. It has never changed at all. But the village people here think that it may be. That's why we live down there on the edge of the town, and that's why I can't find a wife and why my sisters will never find husbands. The brothers here are kind to us. They know it isn't leprosy, so they don't mind buying our vegetables. My older sister goes into the market where people are quite friendly, but I can't. They would throw stones at me. If it troubles you I won't intrude on you again. But it's a lonely life, just the three of us, and no children." He shrugged and turned away... He was just leaving the gate when Josephson called after him, "Lazarus! Lazarus, come back!" The young man turned and looked back across the courtyard. Rather unsteadily Josephson was stumbling over the cobbles towards him. He went back to meet him. Josephson took his arm to steady himself, and smiled to him. "I hope you will come again. I don't think we've finished our conversation. Now help me back to my cell before I fall over." As Lazarus left again, on a sudden impulse Josephson embraced him. The look of surprise and delight on Lazarus' face said it all. His eyes filled with tears. They did have many more conversations.

When Josephson was strong enough to walk down the hill he went to lodge with Lazarus and his two sisters in their guest room so as to leave his cell in the hospice empty for passing visitors. Martha, the older sister, was a handsome but worn-looking woman with traces of grey, Mary some years younger, a pretty girl with raven black hair. Later on, whenever he was passing that way, Josephson lodged with his new friends to avoid the noise and crowds of Jerusalem. Martha always fed him proper meals and Mary sat in the corner listening to him and her brother as they talked long into the evening. About the Restoration of Israel. About God's Kingdom. About Messiah.

V

There was a lot to talk about. Recently the streets and shops were buzzing with excited rumours. Martha reported that there was yet another fiery new prophet down by the Jordan, announcing the imminent arrival of the Messiah and the coming of the Kingdom of God. Josephson decided to make a detour to go down to visit his friends in the Salt Sea communities to find out what was going on. There was an unusually large number of people walking or riding the same way down the steep hill into the valley. When he eventually found Nathanael he discovered that all the community houses were full up with pilgrims heading for the upper Jordan. He slept the night on a fleece on Nathanael's cell floor and gladly joined in the familiar morning rituals of washing and prayer and the communal breakfast of rye bread and goat's cheese.

When they got back to Nathanael's cell he asked about the new prophet who was causing such a stir. "Well, I haven't heard him preaching myself – I can't walk that far these days. But some of the brothers here have been going up regularly to listen to him and say he's drawing huge crowds. Stands up on a big rock beside the river and yells at them like one of the old prophets – just like Elijah, they're saying. Says the Messianic Age is going to begin soon and everyone must clean up their lives if they want to be ready for the Restoration of Israel. And they're listening, really listening. Young James here says it's like he holds them spellbound.

He preaches in the morning and then spends the afternoon baptising those wanting to repent and join up. Great queues of folk, men women and children lining up to get dunked in the river. Even some soldiers and priests. He's pretty stern with them. Calls them snakes and scorpions! But everyone is sure he's been sent by God with a message: the Word of the Lord! He's even accused King Herod of incest! The whole place is fizzing and many of the brothers here are joining up. They say it's what we've all been waiting for all these years. I don't know. Wait and see. Rome will soon start to sit up and take notice. The last time it ended in a blood bath." Josephson asked him what he made of the prophet Daniel. "He says Messiah will come "on the clouds of Heaven" doesn't he? What does that mean?" "Wait and see, my friend. Wait and see. It's all in the Lord's hands, Blessed be He. Why don't you go up there and listen to him. Come back and tell me what you think".

The following day the track up the West bank of the river was crowded with people all heading the same way. Most of them were poor folk, chattering excitedly about the new prophet and the Restoration of Israel and the Coming of the Messiah. Josephson joined a group of brothers from the Community who had been coming up regularly to listen to the Prophet John. Some were even wondering whether he indeed might be the Messiah. Others said that he had been challenged by the Temple authorities and had categorically denied it. All he would say was that he was "a voice crying in the wilderness: Make ready, make ready for the coming Messiah!"

There was already a large crowd gathered round the rock from which John was preaching, families sitting on the ground, youngsters perched on the branches of sycamore trees and a wider circle of standing men and women crowding forward to hear him. Josephson and his friends stood at the back and to one side watching this wild-looking orator in profile, his hair tied back in a long black mane that reached down to his waist, his hairy arms bare to the shoulder and his rough sackcloth tunic reaching down only to his knees above his bare feet. His appearance was certainly striking, but his voice was commanding and his oratory spellbinding. He held the crowds in the hollow of his hand. There was a bunch of Priests and Pharisees grouped together at the rear of the crowd, standing out from the rest of the gathering in their distinctive robes and head dresses. John was already in full flow when Josephson and his friends arrived, caustically challenging the Temple officials over the heads of the crowd.

"You lot!" he bellowed, shaking his fist at them, "Yes, you lot, skulking at the back there, what in God's name are you doing here? Think you can escape Messiah's vengeance by having a dip in the Jordan, do you? You bunch of adders! Unless you clean up your lives and produce the fruits of repentance he'll chop the whole tree down. Here and now the axe is being wielded against the root of your fruitless fig tree!" There were wild cheers and Hosannas from the crowds

"What are you cheering for, you dimwits. The Word of the Lord is to you too! He's on his way, the One who is to come. Think you can leave it until tomorrow, you witless morons? Tomorrow will be too late. What does Holy Scripture tell us? Repent while it is still called 'today'. He's coming to this threshing floor, right here, with his winnowing fan, to throw you lot sky high and God's wind will blow away the sinful chaff and then he'll gather the good grain into his Kingdom. Come down to the river all of you and let the Spirit wash away your sins!"

All around him Josephson saw men and women with tears on their cheeks stretching out their arms towards the mesmerising Prophet, and crying Hosanna! Hosanna! Save us! Save us!" Some, men and women, were lying prostrate. The group of Temple officials seemed to have disappeared. One of his friends whispered in Josephson's ear, "I expect they've gone off to consult the lawyers so they can find texts which prove he's a fraud." "What do you think?" "I don't know. But I'm going to join up because he's really touched my heart. Nothing like this has happened in my lifetime before. Perhaps it is the promised Time. We've waited so long!"

Josephson stepped back. He found the seething crowds shoving him aside and pushing forward confusing and exhausting. He needed time to think, time to get in touch with the inner silence which he now carried with him most of the time. He sat down with a friend in a patch of shade as sections of the crowd struggled down the bank to where John was standing up to his waist in the river with two assistants, pushing men women and children under the surface and then hauling them up and giving them a blessing. Others were beginning to wander away. Some of the newly baptised started singing a psalm. He found it profoundly moving. Surely, surely, this must be what the beginning of the Restoration of Israel would look like? He had no doubt in his mind that John was speaking the Word of the Lord; he too had been communing with the enfolding Presence up there in the cliffs and their caves. There really was something from beyond in him.

The crowds thinned out as the afternoon wore on. Josephson's friend said he would come back tomorrow if he wanted to join him. He shook his head. "No. Not tomorrow. It has to be now, while it is still called today." He got up and walked down into the river.

VI

He found himself lying on his back gazing up into the faces of John and one of his disciples against the sky, looking down anxiously at him. He smiled up at them. He was immersed in a huge, enfolding happiness. Those earlier moments of intense joy, when the world had gone still, had each lasted only a timeless second. This was different. He looked up at John and the young man beside him and felt an overwhelming love for them, this gaunt, craggy man with his deep set eyes and wild hair and beard, and the nervous young man who still had his arm under Josephson's shoulders. They must have carried him bodily out of the river and onto the bank. He felt a surge of intense love for the two of them. He reached up and stroked the young man's face. The lad drew back, startled and uneasy. Then John bent down, took his arm and helped him to his feet. For a long moment they looked deeply into each other's eyes. Josephson smiled and then embraced the older man and quietly said his name. "John!" "Who are you, my friend? What's your name?" Josephson looked up at him and just smiled.

With a hand on John' shoulder he turned and looked round. There was a small fascinated crowd watching this little drama. Josephson felt the same all-enfolding love flowing out for them, the women and puzzled children hanging onto their skirts, the men, some old and grizzled, some young labourers, some clearly disciples from the

Salt Sea communities, a couple of Temple scribes. The whole valley, the river, the trees, the swifts screaming in the evening sky, the patient donkeys, were infinitely beautiful and infinitely precious. And suddenly he knew himself to be infinitely beautiful and precious as well. His friend from the Community walked back with him through the gathering dusk. He asked him if he was all right? What had happened to him? Was he strong enough to get home? Josephson took his arm and smiled at him, "All is well. Everything is well. Blessed be He, the Holy One. Blessed be He."

Next morning he packed up a satchel of bread, a cheese, a knife, a skin of water, and a jar of hot charcoals, and then as an afterthought, his old sling. He told Nathanael that he had to go up to the cave and think. The older man looked at him with his head on one side. "Something has happened, hasn't it? Are you all right? What did you make of John? Is he speaking the Word of the Lord?" Josephson just looked at him and smiled and nodded. And that was all.

The overhanging rock and the cave were as he remembered them. There was no smell of a wild animal, but he picked up a couple of stones just in case. The rough bed of grass, aromatic stems and leaves which he had made on his earlier visits was still there. He put his satchel, his old sling and the skin of water on a shelf of rock at the back of the cave, and went out along the steep bank picking up dead twigs and the occasional withered branch of juniper or wild fig bushes. Further on there was a recent landslide of rock which had uprooted a number of shrubs and small trees. He dragged his treasure trove of firewood back to the mouth of the cave, fed his charcoals with some chips of wood and sat down in the shade.

Now he had time to sit still, the silence engulfed him. All he was aware of was an all – embracing Presence. The intensity of overwhelming happiness was greater than anything he had ever experienced. Those fleeting moments of stillness which had come to him from time to time were like glimpses of sunshine on a cloudy day. This was the unclouded glory of unquenchable light. Unbidden, the words of the great psalms of praise poured from his lips:

Praise the Lord! O praise the Lord!
How good it is to sing praises to our God!
For He is good and a song of praise is His due.
The Lord builds up Jerusalem.
He gathers the outcasts of Israel,
He heals the broken hearted.
And binds up the wounded.
He counts the number of the stars,
And calls them all by their names.

Over the following days he fell into a quiet routine. Rising early he would greet the sunrise with a hymn of praise. On this east side of the valley the first hints of dawn appeared when the cliffs on the far side turned red, then amber in the sudden sunshine. Before the heat of the day he would scramble down the slope to fill his water skin from the stream which ran from a mountain spring at the bottom of the valley. Occasionally he found a group of travellers camped down there who gave him some supplies in exchange for his attention to their animals. Then he would climb back up to his cave and the shadow of the overhanging rock and let the silence enfold him. It held him like his mother's arms.

The Restoration of Israel! It was surely coming, and he would be involved. But what would it mean for all his family and friends? For the crowded streets in Jerusalem? For that poor bruised girl and her baby? For the Temple and its self-confident Priests and stern Pharisees? For the argumentative communities down by the Salt Sea? For his friends by the Sea? For the shepherds up on Hermon and their silly women folk? Would a leader arrive to lead a rebellion against the Romans? That way, surely, was madness. They had tried it in the past and it ended in slaughter.

Unless. Unless God intervened and sent "One like the Son of Man" wielding overwhelming Divine Power. O the thrill of it! At last, at last! Freedom in the newly purified Promised Land. The Presence was here! It was going to fill the Temple again. Would he himself "see the Lord" as Isaiah had? He could feel it like an impending thunderstorm. It was almost as if God was about to crack open the sky above the valley and let loose legions of angels to sweep away the Gentile invaders and cleanse the land, standing with drawn swords on all its borders to repel even Caesar and his mighty armies. But how much blood? How much blood!

He sat in the shadow letting the Presence wrap itself round him. It was utterly awesome, this attentive love which marshals all the stars, and yet was as close as his own breathing. He watched a lizard sunning itself on a ledge outside the cave, and knew that the lizard too was enfolded in love and the ant which scuttled away into a crevice, that too enfolded in love.

Later in the afternoon the setting sun shone right into the cave and he found his way back into the furthest recess. There, tucked in behind a slab of rock, he spotted the neck of a pottery jar. He reached down and hauled it out. It was closed with a disc of wood wrapped in a piece of cloth. He recognised it as like one which Nathaniel had once brought up with him. He carried it out into the evening sunlight and prized the wooden lid open. Inside there were half a dozen papyrus scrolls. Carefully he lifted one out. On the outside it had a label: 'Psalms'. He carefully unrolled it on a flat rock surface. The first turn of the scroll was torn and more or less illegible. But the next bit was beautifully clear, written perhaps by one of the scribes down in the Salt Sea Community. As the sun began to set he ran his finger along a line of text:

I will tell of the decree of the Lord: He said to me, "You are my son: today I have begotten you. Ask of me and I will make the nations your heritage, and the ends of the earth your possession".

He stood transfixed. It felt as if the words had been spoken aloud to him, addressed to him alone. He stared at the text until the sun went down and the sudden dusk shrouded him. Carefully rolling up the scroll he tucked it back in the jar, then he went and stood in the mouth of the cave until the stars began to flicker overhead. He looked up into the darkening sky and whispered, "Abba!" In the silence he seemed to hear a responding whisper, "My son!" and a flood of exultation flowed through him. Late into the night he stood above the valley feeling waves of empowering joy coursing through his veins. So this was the beginning of the Restoration of Israel – this was his vocation, this is what for thirty years he had been waiting for. With a quiet sense of huge endowment and a looming destiny he lay down on his rustling bedding and fell asleep.

The sun was well up when he woke after a long dreamless night. The sense of new energy beating through his veins was exhilarating. His morning praises flowed in joyous song. All those years of searching and questioning were culminating in a surge of new self-confidence. He repeated over and over again the single word *"Abba!"* The valley enfolded him in love. He looked at everything with a responding love, every leaf and withered grass stem, every drifting cloud above the valley, the rock doves on the cliffs, and loved them.

On a sudden impulse he started to climb the steep slope above his cave. In some places he had to scramble on hands and knees, and cascades of loose stones tumbled away below him. He followed the tracks made by the wild goats sometimes along ledges hardly wide enough for him to keep a foothold. He had no fear of falling, and murmured to himself, "*He shall give his angels charge over you lest you hurt your foot against a stone*". And then on one narrow ledge he missed his footing and just managed to grab a projecting rock to save himself from falling into the chasm below. He sat down on a grassy patch and found himself sweating and shaking. So, yes, Abba would care for him, but that didn't mean he needn't take care of himself. When he recovered his breath he climbed on more cautiously. At last the hillside flattened out and he sat down panting at the top of the cliff and looked back.

It seemed as if the whole world was laid out at his feet, immense distances of craggy wilderness disappearing into the blue haze to the south, and far off to the north the silver streak of Jordan and the Salt Sea and there, beyond, the hills above Jerusalem. This is where the Restoration of Israel is beginning – beginning now. This is the chosen place Abba is going to repossess for Himself – his beloved land, His Kingdom. Standing there in the morning glory he felt a surge of love reaching out to the whole world.

The heat of the sun reflected back off the rocks was intense. He scrambled down to where a leaning crag offered a patch of shade, and as he sat down was startled by a snarl to find he was sharing it with a vixen. As she struggled to get up he realised that one of her legs was caught in a snare. He felt a pang of pity for the creature. Yes, a malodorous unclean fox, but Noah had taken two into the Ark, hadn't he? He sat still and tried to soothe her by talking to her quietly. He poured some water from his jar into his cupped hand and held it out to her. She flopped down and lapped at it eagerly. She let him stroke her but pulled away when he touched her leg. Then he felt the familiar tingle up his spine and the sudden warmth in his hands. He whispered, "Abba! This is your creature!" Then quite firmly he put his hand over the animal's leg and closed his eyes, feeling the power pouring down his arm. He loosened the noose and slipped it over her paw. In her struggles she had pulled it tight and the leg was bloody and swollen. She let him hold her leg for a long moment and then pulled away to lick the wound. When he opened his eyes the fox was standing up. It turned to look at him and then limped away down the track. He was tired and thirsty when he finally got back to the coolness of his cave. There was hardly enough water left in his water skin to quench his thirst. He would have to go down to the stream in the morning.

He lay down but was too disturbed and too exhilarated to sleep. The fox. That sudden pang of pity. The surge of power in his hands. He had always known he could help injured beasts, but this was different. It felt as if he was channelling a tenderness which enfolded everything. Now it was enfolding him and soothing the tiredness in his bones. Much later he fell asleep.

VII

He woke wonderfully refreshed. There was a wild goat on the track down the slope with two kids at its heels. He squatted down and called to it softly. It stopped and looked back at him. Then it tossed its head and led the kids off the track into the thicket of scrub. When he got down to the stream he found some mules tied up in the shade of a tree. A group of men and women was clustered on the edge of the stream. One man was holding a boy while a woman bathed his leg. They looked up nervously as he approached. A man put his hand to the hilt of his sword.

Josephson greeted them with a smile. "Peace and blessings be upon you. What's up with the lad?" The boy's ankle was a nasty purple and badly swollen. They said he had sprained it the day before and now he couldn't even put his foot to the ground. Josephson knelt down beside the lad and cradled his ankle in his hands. The now familiar tingle crept down his spine, and the heat surged into the palms of his hands. He looked up at the cliff towering above them and then at the sky, and whispered, "*Abba!*". As he gently stroked it he felt the swelling diminishing. After five minutes the bruising had almost disappeared. He waited until the heat in his hands had faded, and then helped the boy to his feet. Tentatively he took a couple of steps and then looked up at Josephson. "Thank you sir, thank you very much!" "Don't thank me, lad, thank the Lord and bless his Name." There were shouts of amazement. The family all gathered round chattering excitedly. A young woman picked up his water skin and went to the stream to fill it. When the boy's father reached into his tunic for his purse Josephson waved it away. But they pressed food on him, filling his satchel with bread, olives, goats' cheese and dried figs, thanking him profusely. An old man with a long white beard quoted bits of psalms.

Josephson blessed them and left with a farewell greeting. "Peace for your journey. God go with you." As he panted back up the steep track he spotted the wild goat and her kids nibbling the sparse grass under the scrub along the slope. He called quietly to her. She looked up at him while the kids nuzzled at her udder, but returned to her nibbling apparently quite unconcerned by his presence. Back in the cool of the cave, he sat down against the cold stone of the wall and let the silence enfold him. The sense of Presence was almost overwhelming. He thought back to the previous day. What was it that had prompted him to take that dangerous goats' track up the cliff side? How was it that there was that projection of rock just there to save him when he almost fell? What was that stirring in his soul as he surveyed the world from the cliff top with such ecstatic joy? What was it that responded to his unspoken prayer and healed the vixen's wounded leg? What was the sudden surge of heat which cured the boy's swollen ankle under his hands? Where did the power come from? He had looked up to the sky, hadn't he, and invoked the name Abba. He had often looked up at the stars and spoken the same name. But the Presence wasn't up there. It was here in the cave. No. Not in the sky or the stars or the cave but inside the silence in his own soul.

An image from his childhood came into his mind. A lined black face with crinkles of laughter round her eyes saying quietly to him, "Well there's your miracle, my boy!" And in front of him the newly dug well at Nazareth full of crystal clear water from the hidden spring. Slowly, almost timidly, he reached down into the inner stillness in his heart as if seeking to find the pulse and throb of this spring of power and joy which seemed to be seeping up into his life. Yes! There! No, here! Closer to him than his own breathing. Abba was here, in his heart.

He had no idea how long that moment of inner revelation lasted, but when the numbness in his leg forced him to stir and get up the sun was already beginning to shine into the mouth of his cave. He took a gulp of water from his gourd, and thought of the well at Nazareth. A deep breath of the warm afternoon air was heavy with all the aromatic scents of the mountain shrubs, and he found himself murmuring, "Abba! Abba! Abba!" Yes, here, closer to him than his own breathing! A constant spring of water in his own heart! He turned back into the cave where the light of the setting sun was streaming along the inner wall, highlighting all the lumps and hollows and fissures in the rock face. As he walked back his eye was suddenly caught by two lumps protruding from the wall and two curved ridges – yes horns! Bit by bit the huge beast pieced itself together, the head and two deep eyes, a massive forehead and below the receding forequarters of an enormous bull leaping out of the wall from another world. In terror he exclaimed aloud "Abba!", stepped back and tripped. When he stumbled to his feet the shadows had moved on and the illusion had vanished. He shook his head and then remembered that he had come to look for something. He was trying to recall the words of a psalm Rabbi Reuben used to quote, that was it. He went to find the scroll in Nathaniel's urn, and unrolled it on the sunlit rock at the cave mouth until he came to the half- remembered text. He ran his fingers along the fading lines of script. As he read he whispered the words aloud, just as Reuben had taught him to. The stillness crept up on him and in the silence he knew he was speaking to the enfolding Presence.

O LORD, you have searched me and known me. You know when I sit down and when I rise up; you discern my thoughts from far away. You search out my path and my lying down, and are acquainted with all my ways. Even before a word is on my tongue, LORD, you know it completely. You hem me in, behind and before, and lay your hand upon me. Such knowledge is too wonderful for me; it is so high that I cannot attain it.

Where can I go from your spirit? Or where can I flee from your presence? If I ascend to heaven, you are there; if I make my bed in Sheol, you are there. If I take the wings of the morning and settle at the farthest limits of the sea, even there your hand shall lead me, and your right hand shall hold me fast. If I say, "Surely the darkness shall cover me, and the light around me become night", even the darkness is not dark to you; the night is as bright as the day, for darkness is as light to you. For it was you who formed my inward parts; you knit me together in my mother's womb. I praise you, for I am fearfully and wonderfully made.

Wonderful are your works; that I know very well. My frame was not hidden from you, when I was being made in secret, intricately woven in the depths of the earth. Your eyes beheld my unformed substance. In your book were written all the days that were formed for me, when none of them as yet existed. How weighty to me are your thoughts, O God! How vast is the sum of them! I try to count them – they are more than the sand; when I come to the end – I am still with you.

He stood there in the light of the setting sun completely spellbound, wrapped in the enfolding love. He felt a vast tenderness embracing him and everything, the cliffs, the wild goats, the shrubs and screes, and the swifts circling above the valley. A vixen yelped somewhere below him and he felt a finger of love reach out to her and her cubs. He murmured "Abba, you bless the world." Then he bent over the scroll again and moved his finger on to trace the line.

O that you would kill the wicked, O God, and that the bloodthirsty would depart from me – those who speak of you maliciously, and lift themselves up against you for evil! Do I not hate those who hate you, O Lord? And do I not loathe those who rise up against you? I hate them with perfect hatred; I count them my enemies.

He stood back, feeling he had been struck in the face. The moments of silent ecstasy were shattered like a falling pot. It was Holy Scripture but it felt like a blasphemy. The Bull! He had a shuddering sense that there was another awesome presence behind the wall, an immense power. Yes, that was what the Restoration of Israel needed. Power to cleanse the Land! He felt a thrill of excitement in his veins.

He woke before dawn, after a restless night full of strange dreams and half waking fears. The vixen screamed again in the distance, but now it was a sound of horror. What had it killed this night? So all his warm feelings of being enfolded in love by the divine Presence were just illusions? Seductions to tempt him to doubt the Holy Word of God? The rage he had felt up on Hermon at those silly women with their flowers for the Goddess, was that really what Abba felt for them too, a huge purifying fire? Such power! As the sun struck the top of the cliffs on the far side of the valley he moved out onto the level ledge in front of the cave. The air out here was still cold from the night chill; he shivered and turned back to find his cloak. As he did so he found himself facing a young leopard standing motionless twenty yards along the track. For a long minute the young man and the wild beast stood stock still looking into each others' eyes. When he stooped to grab a stone she snarled at him and slipped away up the hillside. She was very thin, and limping. He found himself shivering partly from cold and partly from fright. He busied himself with stirring up the charcoal in his jar and feeding it with dry grass and twigs until it burst into flame. He lit the fire on the ashes at the threshold of the cave, cut off a hunk of dry bread and a bit of goat's cheese and then sat beside the fire to warm his chilled bones.

As the sun crept down the far cliffs, he reached out to find the enfolding Presence, but the valley was dry and empty. Parched and lifeless. He reached down inside himself, but his soul was as dry as an empty gourd. Was it all a bad dream, this vision of the Restoration of Israel; that overwhelming sense of being immersed in the Spirit, when John carried him up from the river; the voice from the scroll which called him "My son"? A carpenter's son from Nazareth? A wandering dreamer? He shook his fist at the sky. Then, realising how thirsty he was, he picked up his water skin and satchel, found the sling where he had dumped it at the back of the cave, and set off down the track. He paused to pick up some stones. Half way down the scree the wild goat skittered away, with only one kid at her heels, and he remembered hearing the fox screeching in the night. Poor creature. There was a group of people encamped by the stream and as he came down the slope someone spotted him and cried out. There was an immediate bustle, and people began hurrying towards him, some of them carrying children in their arms, a young man with an old woman on his back, and at the back a lone woman, veiled and limping on a stick with no one near her.

He recognised some of them from his last visit to the stream. The same girl came and took his water skin, and a man lifted his satchel off his shoulder with a welcoming smile. He sat down on a rock and looked up at the empty sky. All he could do was to murmur "Abba! Abba!". He let a young man place a child on his lap, and immediately the familiar tingling ran down his spine, and the burning sensation in his hands became intense. The child was clearly feverish and whimpered as he touched him, but he quietened as Josephson held him, and stopped shivering. He spent the morning with the little group and their animals, and then, as he was about to leave, he noticed the solitary woman with the veil over her head. When he beckoned to her the little crowd moved away from them, but stood watching. She came and squatted on the ground a couple of yards away from him.

Josephson greeted her, "Peace be with you, my daughter." Hesitantly she lifted her veil and turned her face away. One cheek was disfigured by a wide purple blotch, exactly like the mark on his friend Lazarus's face. The tingling up his back returned and the hair rose on the nape of his neck... He reached out to her and helped her to her feet, and placed his hand over the mark. At that moment the valley was inundated with the enfolding Presence. "Peace be upon you, daughter. Have you had this since you were born?" She nodded speechlessly. "Then it is not leprosy. Go to the priests and tell them you were born with this mark." He turned to the watching men and women. "This is not leprosy. You have nothing to fear from her. You must care for her. She is a daughter of Abraham, a child of God's Kingdom." The young woman who had filled his water skin, went hesitantly up to the disfigured woman and took her hand. The woman burst into tears as they gathered round her. Clambering back up the steep cliff path, Josephson felt a wave of relief and joy. Only God, surely only his loving Abba, could work such a transformation. It was true after all. The Restoration of Israel was beginning. And Abba really had named him as the One who was to start the transformation of the world. Not the Bull.

Half way up the path he heard a sudden buzz of flies. He looked under a bush and saw the body of the goat's other kid. It was partly mangled, its throat torn out and its belly ripped open, and covered with flies. He waved them away, and picked it up by its back legs. It was still stiff, so not long killed. He could get two or three meals off this pathetic little corpse. He skinned and jointed the animal, fed the fire and propped up a branch of juniper to act as a spit. The cave was filled with the smell of roasting meat and the aromatic smoke from the juniper. He sat down in the mouth of the cave and watched the sun go down behind the opposite hills. He did not bother to look behind him at the cave wall. Yes, maybe there are other presences, but the only one who spoke to him was Abba. He recited an evening psalm and waited for the silence to settle around him.

What was he being told? The Restoration of Israel was coming, and he was going to be part of that Coming. But what kind of Restoration? The Salt Sea communities spoke of a purifying of the land, as did the Pharisees. God would destroy the sinners. He had noticed that many of the fisher folk down by the Lake didn't bother with the ritual hand-washing before eating, which Rabbi Reuben had insisted on, but they were good honest folk and looked after their neighbours. Would they be purged? They were "sinners" according to the Pharisees. That fat old priest in the Temple probably kept all the ritual regulations, but was a loathsome man. That bruised girl with the baby had probably become a prostitute by now. Soiled goods. No one would take her in now. And her baby? Poor little child.

He got up and turned the juniper branch over. The smell of roasting meat made his mouth water. When he came to purify the land, how was Messiah going to tell the good and the bad apart? Everyone was such a mixture. The priests said that his friend Lazarus was a leper because either he or his parents had committed some dreadful sin. But he was a lovable man, and he said his mother and father were good people too. How far back did the fatal fault lie? But, surely, the prophet had said everyone must answer for their own sins, hadn't he? And the animals, what about them? Some were clean, some were impure. That was Torah. Would the destroying angel kill all the pigs and all the Roman soldiers? The kids called the legionaries "pigs!" His Gentile friends told him that roast piglet was delicious. And then Reuben had told him about a Roman centurion who had learned their language and helped re-roof the synagogue. What about him? And the fanatical Zealots who made a virtue of knifing Roman soldiers in the dark streets, some just teenagers on their first tour of duty. And behind all this muddle there was the Holy Torah, the Scriptural bedrock of Israel, the great stone tablets with God's own words chiselled into the granite. Josephson knew much of the Torah by heart. But here in the enfolding silence of this stony valley the Presence which had rescued Israel from slavery in Egypt was stirring in his soul and enfolding him, speaking to him different words. New words. Was it like this for Moses? Did He speak to Moses like this?

The kid's fat was beginning to burn in the fire. He lifted it off on the aromatic juniper branch, laid it on the flat rock at the cave mouth, and cut a sizzling chunk off its haunch. Some sharp instinct made him look up. He sensed he was being watched. It was dark outside but in the light of the fire he could see two green eyes watching him. Instinctively he reached down for a stone, and then paused. That young leopard, you could see every rib under her skin. And she was lame. He cut most of the meat off the still warm bone and then tossed it out to where the leopard had been crouching. He took the remains of the meat to the back of the cave and then built up the fire. Somewhere outside in the darkness he could hear a bone being scrunched. He smiled and blessed the Lord.

The kid lasted Josephson and the leopard two days. She still snarled at him when he came too close, but he was confident that she wasn't going to attack him. She seemed to see him as a possibly harmless source of an occasional snack. He talked quietly to her whenever she limped up to his ledge under the overhanging rock, and poured some of his precious water into a hollow in a rock and stood back in the cave to watch her when she ventured up to lap at it. What was he being told? Abba loved this creature? A man-eating leopard! And the dead kid which had kept them both alive? And the vixen which he had released from that cruel snare? She had gone on to kill the kid. What a strange love. That poor girl and the baby she had probably lost, and the silly women going up the mountain with their flowers for Astarte, and his friend Lazarus and his sisters, and, yes, even that fat cynical old priest in the Temple – and the rough Roman soldiers, were they too all embraced in this enfolding love? He sat in the stillness and let his heart drift down into that inner place where the water flowed. Yes, they too were held in being by this strange Love. And these thoughts welling up inside him? Yes, they too were flowing from that inner spring. He whispered "*Abba! Abba! Father of all things!*" Somewhere deep inside him there was an answering whisper, "*My son.*"

The next morning the leopard was crouching by the track when he came out to chant his morning psalm. He put the remains of the meat which was to be his breakfast onto a rock beside him and called to her. Very cautiously she sidled up, grabbed the meat and backed away. Her leg was visibly swollen and she could hardly put it to the ground. He talked quietly to her and held out his hand with the last bit of meat She took it from him and he let her sniff at his hand. Then she licked it with her rough tongue. He purred and she purred back. She let him stroke her. When he put his hand down to her paw she growled at him, but she let him hold it. The now familiar warmth coursed down his arm and the hair rose up on the back of his neck. He sat there with animal's leg in his hand until the heat of the sun reached them over the brow of the hill. Then gently he let go and she licked her paw then backed away, limping but walking confidently on the injured leg. He never saw her again.

VIII

It was from that day that he began to listen for the inner voice more attentively. On one day when his water ran out and he had very little left to eat he started off down to the stream when something brought him to a halt. He went back into the cave and sat in the silence all day. It was only on the third day that the silence lifted and with a raging thirst and famished with hunger he was released to go down the track. There was a small gathering of folk waiting for him down there. He quenched his thirst from the stream, washed his face and feet and turned to find them all gathered round. They looked anxious and nervous. Apparently a gang had been robbing travellers along the road further up the valley the previous day and a man had been killed. Josephson attended to their needs and they put some bread and cheese into his satchel and filled his water skin for him, but were anxious to move on before it got dark. He blessed them, and watched them disappear up the road.

When the Restoration of Israel came would all this violence be ended? But how? Violence breeds more violence. Rome knew that but never learned. The questions haunted him all the way up to his cave. The wild goat was browsing beside the track. She bleated, but there was no sign of the other kid. He wondered whether the leopard had killed it, now she could hunt again. The goat took a hunk of bread from his hand and followed him up the steep track. Next morning he was woken by the goat bleating. He gave her a piece of bread and then noticed her swollen udder. He fetched Nathaniel's jar, carefully extracted the scrolls, and after a bit of nervous backing away she let him milk her. He rewarded her with some more bread and she ambled off up the track. He blessed the Lord for her warm milk, yes, for a land flowing with milk and honey. Then picked up one of the scrolls and unrolled it.

It was marked "Isaiah". Nathanael had revered the prophet of the Exile, calling him the one who saw the future most clearly. Josephson read on from the middle of the scroll where it fell open on the flat rock and as he read he felt his heart beating faster. It was about the Servant, the One who would come, the One who would redeem God's people. Could Isaiah answer his questions? The sense of enfolding Presence became suddenly acute, as if this text was given to him at this moment in this place. Everything had converged to this moment, all the random events of the past days were like stepping stones across a stream – the wild beasts, the travellers in the valley who kept him supplied, the growing awareness of Abba's enfolding and guiding love. And now, this text.

For he grew up before him like a young plant, and like a root out of dry ground; he had no form or majesty that we should look at him, nothing in his appearance that we should desire him. He was despised and rejected by others; a man of suffering and acquainted with infirmity; and as one from whom others hide their faces he was despised, and we held him of no account. Surely he has borne our infirmities and carried our diseases; yet we accounted him stricken, struck down by

God, and afflicted. But he was wounded for our transgressions, crushed for our iniquities; upon him was the punishment that made us whole, and by his bruises we are healed.

Well, well. He smiled grimly. That fitted him well enough. He knew about infirmities and diseases sure enough, and was a head shorter than his brothers. He read on.

All we like sheep have gone astray; we have all turned to our own way, and the Lord has laid on him the iniquity of us all. He was oppressed, and he was afflicted, yet he did not open his mouth; like a lamb that is led to the slaughter, and like a sheep that before its shearers is silent, so he did not open his mouth. By a perversion of justice he was taken away. Who could have imagined his future? For he was cut off from the land of the living, stricken for the transgression of my people. They made his grave with the wicked and his tomb with the rich although he had done no violence, and there was no deceit in his mouth.

Josephson stood transfixed. A cold shiver ran down his spine. Was this really what Isaiah saw as the destiny of the Servant? The prophet who Nathanael used to say "saw the future more clearly than any". But what about the Restoration of Israel? What about "The Son of Man coming with the Clouds of Heaven,"? What about Messiah arriving surrounded by the Lord's *Shekinah*? What about the legions of angels who were going to come with him to purify the Promised Land? What about Abba, who he imagined had called him His dear son? It was all too confusing and agonising. He clenched his fists and cried out a harsh animal cry of despair. Were all his lovely dreams and visions illusions? Perhaps worse, demonic temptations. The Bull? Standing in the dusk at the entrance to his cave he lifted his arms to the sky and cried out "Abba! Oh, Abba!, Help me! Help me!" There was no answer, no Presence, only a mocking echo from the far cliffs. A flock of rock doves took off from a crevice above him and circled the valley before coming back to their roosting place with a flurry of wings. He said an evening psalm to an empty sky.

After a restless night he slept heavily before dawn and woke to find the sun brilliant on the far cliffs. His mouth was dry and his water skin was empty. He struggled stiffly to his feet feeling a deep ache in his hip – he must have lain awkwardly on it as he slept. Limping a bit he made his way down to the stream to be met by half a dozen men and women who greeted him excitedly. The woman with the birthmark had been to the Temple and the priests had declared her clean and her birthmark seemed to be fading and her family had taken her back into their house. They pressed food onto him but he had forgotten to bring his satchel down with him. One of the women gave him her own bag full of provisions and they filled his water skin for him. As they were leaving, almost as an afterthought he asked them about John's ministry of Baptism by the Jordan. They looked at him in surprise. "Haven't you heard? Herod has thrown him into prison! And his followers have all gone into hiding. He went a bit too far with all his attacks on Herod's marriage. There's no one down by the river now." So, that is what happens to anyone who is called to proclaim the Restoration of Israel. Isaiah was right.

It was intolerably close down by the stream, with not a breath of air, and the sky was dark with towering clouds. He was drenched in sweat as he struggled up the track with his heavy water skin and bag of provisions. By the time he reached his cave he had a throbbing headache, as he sometimes did before a thunder storm, and his leg was painful. It was a little cooler up there and there was an occasional gust of wind which blew the dead leaves up into the air. He took a gulp of water and lay down on his straw bed. He was woken later by a great crash of thunder, and he remembered that other time – it seemed so long ago – when he had sung with joy the praises of the Lord, the God of storms. Wearily he got up and went to stand in the mouth of the cave. The centre of the storm seemed to be further down the valley this time, but the cliffs were ablaze with constant flashes of lightning. When the rain came, it came in a sudden deluge and he stepped back under cover, out of the cascade pouring over his overhanging rock. When it was over and the thunder rumbling away to the South there was a wonderful freshness on the air and it seemed as if all the aromatic herbs and shrubs of this dry land had released their perfumes into the cool of the night. All around him there were trickles and rivulets of water seeping into the fissures and crannies in the rocks and soaking the pockets of dry soil all the way down to the stream. It had happened once before when he was up here and three days later the whole mountain side had been sprinkled with tufts of new grass and sudden splashes of red and yellow flowers. The seeds must have been waiting for months, perhaps for years, for this refreshing downpour to restore them to life. Restoration! Was this what the Restoration of Israel really meant? The thunder and lightning of God's Holiness and the outpouring of grace and mercy onto a parched land. And seeds waiting for God's rain.

How could you hold those two in your head at the same time? He had dreamt once that he was standing on a hill looking down on a city with a huge pagan temple at its centre, when a black thunder cloud rolled over it darkening the whole land. Out of the heart of the cloud a blinding shaft of lightning struck straight down. When the sky cleared the temple and all the buildings round it were a ruin of rubble. His first thought was, How many innocent women and children had died in the conflagration? Where was Abba? It was all so confusing.

He sat on his flat rock and let the creeping silence enfold him. He had to think, and to trust that his thinking was being guided by the hidden Presence of his silent Abba.

Lead me, Lord, lead me in your righteousness and make your way plain before my feet.

He *must* work his way through this tangle of voices and visions and yearnings. Yes, he was being called to begin the Restoration of Israel. He was sure of that. And now John was in Herod's cruel dungeon it was time to grasp his destiny, whatever it turned out to be. So many voices! Daniel's vision of a triumphant warrior? The Salt Sea Community hoping for legions of angels and a cleansed Land? The Temple where they said the Holy of Holies held Moses' stone tablets, now polluted by greedy money-changers and venal priests – and the home of demons? It held the Torah written by God himself. But somehow they didn't live the heart of it, loving kindness, mercy, pity, compassion, righteousness, justice, caring for the widow, the orphan and the immigrant. Was all that apparatus of sacrifices, all that blood and death really what God wanted? Yes, it *is* God's Word, but there was so much violence, so many contradictory texts, so much cruelty and hatred. And what about the poor of the land and their unclean ways of life, not wicked but like sheep without a shepherd? What would happen to them? What about Lazarus and his sisters, or the coarse and sometimes blasphemous fisher folk down by the Sea, the lad John, not holy but "as good as bread" as his mother used to say. And the young soldiers trapped in the ruthless machinery of the Roman army. They weren't bad lads. And the poor abused women on the back streets of Jerusalem. Down in Galilee there were thousands of Gentile folk still worshipping the Goddess or other pagan idols. Not wicked folk, not really "unclean" in spite of the Torah's prescriptions, just ignorant. Sheep without a shepherd. When Messiah comes, how will he judge all this confusing mess of humanity? No, that was not the question. The question was, how was Abba going to make such judgements, when he himself was going to proclaim the coming Restoration of Israel?

Almost before he asked the question he knew what the answer had to be. If indeed the voice at his baptism had been true and not a demonic temptation he must call on Abba's enfolding love at every moment and in every place for the rest of his life. He had to *live* Abba's love in Abba's world. That was the only road to Israel's rescue and God's Kingdom. John with all his passionate oratory and his threats had tried and failed. But he couldn't see how Abba's way could possibly succeed. Nevertheless, success or failure, it had to be this way. This enfolding love was what he had experienced as a small child lying in the hayfield and watching a black-and-white spider struggling through the grass stems. The world had gone still and was suddenly awash with radiance. Perhaps, he thought, it was the children who saw that hidden mystery of the world, what all children see until their eyes are closed by Satan, by the pervasive darkness which cannot bear the light. He must go and heal Israel's blindness. He must bind up Israel's running sores. He must straighten Israel's crooked limbs. He must help them find their true selves. Pour Abba's water onto their parched souls. As this sudden calling dawned on him he knew what he must do and felt himself enfolded once again in the flowing tide of Abba's radiance. A great peace filled him, and the world went still.

He woke as the sun came up and touched the crags over the valley. A sense of exultation and excitement filled him. Being a son meant loving forwards with his hand in Abba's hand, just as he had once walked with his hand in Joseph's hand, walking into a new world. He washed his face, ate a breakfast of olives and goat's cheese with a hunk of bread, scattered some crumbs for the rock doves who often visited him, carefully tucked the scrolls back into Nathanael's jar, sealed it up and hid it behind the rock at the back of the cave. Perhaps someone seeking refuge would come and find it one day. He stood looking out over the valley which he had grown to love and sang his morning psalm. Then he picked up his satchel and water skin, decided he didn't need his sling and set off down the steep track for the last time.

There were some rough tents by the stream which was overflowing its banks, but no one was up and about, so he set off up the valley. It was high noon when he came to the Jordan ford. The water was deep after the storms, so he cut himself a strong willow branch to steady himself against the current and stepped into the river.

REFLECTIONS

In the early centuries of Christianity there was an efflorescence of hagiographic stories about Jesus. One of the more engaging ones tells of the child Jesus playing in the street with other village children making mud animals and birds. The other boys were older than him and laughed at the little kid's crude attempt to make clay sparrows. At length the boy was so upset he just touched his sparrows and they all flew up and settled on the roof. But of course! He was Incarnate Deity, wasn't he? It is an instructive tale because it seems clear (at least to a 21st-Century Westerner) that Deity does not confer magical powers. Or does it? What is the transition from turning mud to living sparrows, to the multiplication of bread and fish, or to turning water into Chateau Petrus, or to cursing a fig tree, or to Resurrection? Where do we draw the line?

Television has brought into our homes ingenious conjurers who leave their audiences and us dumbfounded, our mouths open with amazement. We know it must be a trick – the laws of nature do not allow such wonders to be anything but tricks. But, as a thought experiment, suppose we encountered one such "trick" for which no scientific scrutiny could find an explanation, would we attribute it to Divine intervention, particularly if the miracle worker claimed divine powers? Or would we conclude that our scientific knowledge was not yet sufficiently sophisticated to provide a rational explanation? Like dowsing. Or would we attribute it to psychological suggestion?

Our pre-Enlightenment ancestors used Jesus' miracles as proof of his Divinity. We are more inclined to think that miracles of this kind are actually dissuasive of faith. Uri Geller is an interesting case in point. His speciality was bending spoons by stroking them. Sceptics immediately charged him with deception. Television cameras were deployed. The camera men must have been part of the conspiracy to mislead. Eminent public figures were wheeled on as witnesses. They were credulous and scientifically ignorant. So the CIA conducted extensive and carefully supervised tests and concluded that his psychic powers were genuine. It was reluctantly and tacitly agreed that Geller did have unusual faculties, but no one was able to explain them. But he then lost three successive libel cases against an author and publisher who claimed he was a fraud. In the course of all this still unresolved controversy no one suggested that he was a divine being.

The purpose of my little novella about Jesus' "hidden years" is to try and address this issue of the nature of the relationship between the humanity and divinity in Christ. What are the boundaries of our humanity? If someone is superhuman are they still human? There is a parallel issue about his mother. Is Mary superhuman?

All my life I have had a concern about Christianity's presentation of the flesh, bone, blood and brain of Jesus: his humanity. I say presentation because it is images, not concepts, which strike fire from the flint of the human heart. "Humanity" and "Divinity" are abstractions; neither has much imaginative traction. They are more like equations in algebra or particle physics. There is a similar problem with the representation of the Virgin Mary. A sceptical old friend used to talk angrily about his desire to "strip the blue off Mary". The real facts of Mary's humanity surely involved all a normal woman's physical functions: periods, defecation, headaches, blisters, chapped hands, swollen and painful breasts, tiredness, sharp words, and, as she got older, a worn and lined face from bearing, rearing, feeding and clothing a large family. She may well have been a "lovely woman", faithful, kind and generous and a loving wife and mother, but heavily marked by the wear and tear of peasant life. No doubt like almost all women at the time she had lost some babies before they were one year old, and bore the scars of grief.

The early Christians had many disputes about the relationship between Jesus' humanity and his divinity. In distant Alexandria scholarly metaphysicians tended to exalt his Divinity and to down-play his humanity. In Antioch, just over the hill from Galilee, the real earthiness of his humanity was a close, familiar reality. In terms of representation Alexandria won the battle. The earthy humanity of Jesus was inevitably shrouded in the glory of the risen and exalted Saviour, and by osmosis (contagion?) Mary also became shrouded in reflected glory, a quasi-Divine being, *Theotokos*, Mother of God, the object of prayer and veneration, and even, according to some devotees, Co-Redemptrix with Jesus. Such an exalted Being surely could not have been contaminated by such earthy and suspect stuff as sex, so she must have been always *Virgo intacta* – hence the doctrine of the Virgin Birth; in that case the "brothers and sisters" of Jesus mentioned in the Gospels must have been not his siblings but his cousins. The "sanitising" of Mary then has to be extended to her birth too, resulting in the Immaculate Conception, a doctrine which claims that her mother Anna conceived her without the contagion of Original Sin. Miracles multiply exponentially.

Ardent feminists are keen to point out that it was exclusively men – sexually traumatised, celibate men – who painted this picture of an essentially un-erotic woman, and they like to suggest that it was the latent misogyny or gynophobia of a patriarchal culture which has had such dire consequences for the relationship between men and women for two thousand years. Poor Eve never had a chance, and her daughters (did she have any?) have suffered ever since and continue to do so.

The consequence of the sanitising of Mary in Christian devotion has been an almost total absence of representations of the real Mary of Nazareth. The only striking modern figure that I know is the *Walking Madonna* by Elizabeth Frink in the Close at Salisbury Cathedral, a gaunt elderly woman striding out of the Close with extraordinary determination. (There is a local rumour that she is walking out of the Cathedral in exasperation.) For many modern viewers she is a more truthful figure than the usual image of an insipid, pretty (white) young woman robed in blue, adorned with a crown and surrounded by cherubs. This hagiographic gilding of Jesus' mother has nurtured a bountiful efflorescence of popular devotion and learned theology, providing a fruitful balance between male and female images of Divinity, supplementing the dominant patriarchal iconography of the Abrahamic tradition with a softer maternal femininity more associated with the pagan deities like Astarte, Artemis or even Aphrodite. Within living memory travellers in the remote mountains of

Lebanon have found pre-Christian shrines now rededicated to the Virgin who is still known locally as the Great Lady or even the Green Lady, which were titles of Astarte. Later she morphs into *Prima Vera* and the Virgin Queen.

But why does this hagiography endure? As one worshipper explained, her devotion to Mary was "Because she's so human" (unlike Jesus!). In her sanitised form she does offer real consolation and an ideal to many millions of devout Christians. But the victory of Alexandria persists; the humanity of Jesus has been shrouded in his Divinity, and the divinised womanhood of Mary as Mother of God is beyond the reach of ordinary mortals, though not beyond their longings. The Figure of Beatrice in Dante's great poem has long left behind the pretty 16-year-old girl he met in the street and turned her into a glorious Heavenly Being. As Princess Diana tragically demonstrated, real human beings cannot survive the tsunami of human worship. But images of heaven do supply a wonderful kaleidoscope of poetic dreams and feed many spiritual hungers. The Michelangelo *Pieta* is a deeply moving masterpiece of creative imagination that must make the angels weep. But it's not Mary of Nazareth. For many hundreds of years Christians have used the Heavenly Mary as a mystical icon. Yet Jesus prayed that God's Kingdom would come "on earth". We cease to be truly human if we lose our roots in the muddy evolution of Planet Earth. Jesus is just as human as we are, but what more? The "more" has pulled up Mary's roots as well as his.

The question behind my little narrative of the "hidden years" is this: is it possible to give an account of the meaning and effects of the Incarnation in terms which have plausible traction for a modern European mind, terms not involving any metaphors or concepts which are meaningless to anyone unfamiliar with the customary Biblical images or metaphysical categories in which Christian doctrine is traditionally formulated? It may be that the categories of Biblical thinking and the languages of Scripture and Aristotelian metaphysics are intrinsic to the concepts which they connote, rather as (by some accounts) Arabic is the only language in which the Koran can be rightly understood. Christians assert that the Crucifixion of Jesus is uniquely *sui generis,* both historically and theologically, and say that, like a great work of art, it cannot be fully *explained* in any language, but only by transient metaphors; in an important sense it can only be contemplated, just as a musical or theatrical performance has to be not only heard, but *listened to* and intensely *attended to.* It can't be put into words. Is that true of the Incarnation as well? Maybe all we can do is to contemplate a human baby in the hay, who grew up to die in the love of God and change the world. That dying is the key to the mystery of God's love. The Resurrection is an affirmation that there is a pregnant mystery in his death, the interface between Deity and Humanity, which is life-giving love.

Great art can be studied and explicated, its rich symbolisms highlighted and its constructions clarified. In the case of the Crucifixion, to help us to do that, our Christian tradition is steeped in a treasury of concepts and metaphors many of whose cogs, however, simply do not now mesh with our minds: ransom, payment of debt, expiation, sacrifice, remission of sins, substitutionary penalty, oblation, satisfaction and many others. Incarnation has its own set of metaphysical algebras. But can we manage without them?

We want to continue to assert that Christ's death was *for* me, *for* us, or *for* the world. But that heavily loaded little word has several possible meanings. Was it *because of* us? Or *on our behalf*? Or *instead of* us? That last option is fairly alien to our thinking, but with a bit of caution maybe it can stand. In its original historical setting the crucifixion could have meant some of those things quite literally in relation to Jesus' close friends. "I am the man you want. Let these men go". That was *instead* of his friends. It might be said that his death was *because of* the failure of those friends to support him, but more generally it was *because* of the social, political and moral corruption of his own countrymen, and the ruthless imperial machinery of Rome.

But they weren't "us" here and now, two thousand years later. How does his death plausibly have a retrospective cause, "because of us", or direct effects on "us" apart from the emotional tug the *story* has on our lives? Is it simply by its after-effects, like Hiroshima? That changed the world physically and has changed our global culture dramatically, as did the Holocaust. Or is it, as many Christians affirm, because the whole of humanity has been given a new status or meaning in the eyes of the Creator of the Universe, whether we know it or not? There is a moving story from the ancient world of a ship becalmed off the wooded coast of Croatia on the Friday afternoon when Jesus died on Calvary. In the silence of the dead calm the sailors heard a great piercing cry rising from the deep forest: "GREAT PAN HAS DIED!" [Pan was the Universal God of Nature]. That is certainly a grand affirmation, but it does look a bit like a "nice idea", with a long and perplexing entail of further questions.

At the time, the effects of the death of Jesus of Nazareth were negligible, at least in the immediate future. Rome was unmoved; Israel went on in its own doomed way. True, its later after-effects were far from negligible. "Jesus communities" sprang up all over the Mediterranean world. Jerusalem was sacked, Rome pillaged and Christianity became the axle on which Europe turned. Not that those dramatic political events were effects of Calvary, but when they happened Christianity was waiting at the open door to move in. Are we then to say that the meaning and purpose of Christ's death can be construed exhaustively in the light if its later historical consequences? Geographically they have been fairly local, at least until the last two centuries. What about the millions in Imperial China and the teeming ancient kingdoms of South America? The after-effects of the Jesus tsunami have indeed finally reached those remote shores but the linkage of that little "for" between Jerusalem in AD 30, and the Incas in 1400 or Beijing in 2017, seems to ask for something more than a very slow historical tide of cause and effect. The vast majority of the human race has been untouched by it over the past two thousand years, not to mention the untold hominid millions emerging from the Palaeolithic darkness of the distant past. We want to claim it was for them too. (For the moment we can set to one side the possibility that elsewhere in this unimaginably vast Universe there are other intelligent and moral beings. But if they do exist was it *for* them too?)

What did Jesus think his death was *for*? After all, he almost certainly had some idea himself. But before that there is a prior question: what did he think his life was for? The Christian faith tells us that in his *humanity* God's divinity was incarnate. Incarnation is the key to Atonement. It means that the dying of Jesus takes place in two realms. One is in the realm of history; the other in the realm of the omnipresent Love of the Creator for every particle of his creation simultaneously at all times and in all places. John the visionary saw the Lamb at the centre of the Throne of God; that is God's self-sacrifice of love for all his creatures from the beginning of time. How does the Lamb get onto the Throne? By being there before all worlds.

What was his humanity like, this one, local, time-bound human body, mind and heart, which was caught up, immersed in, marinated in the well-spring of the cosmic sacrificial Love of God? Hidden from us he had lived a fully human life for thirty years before he appears on the scene in the Gospel narratives. There are hints and suggestions in the Gospels and in the Epistles, but anything we build on them is going to be largely speculation. Intelligent biographers admit that they can never get right inside their subject's head and heart; there is always a mystery at the centre of every human life, as Hamlet knew. A Roman Catholic historian or novelist will paint a very different portrait of Thomas More from one written by a Protestant author. Jesus would certainly have been using the concepts and images stored up in his inherited Jewish tradition, which we find so awkward and obscure; for him and his followers they were lying ready to hand as keys to the man himself and the dramatic events of his life and death. But the land too, its hills and villages, its flowers and streams, its people, their language, customs, taboos, longings, and limitations must have had a profound effect in shaping the way he saw and responded to the world about him. The Land was in his bones and blood, and he thought in Aramaic, the language of the Land, which has none of the metaphysical algebra of Greek.

In his case the problem is compounded by the fact that those who recorded his sayings and doings were not biographers in any modern sense – they were committed advocates of a particular interpretation of his death, or, to be accurate, a variety of particular interpretations. Did they read back into his mind and put into his mouth their own later convictions about his significance in the religious cosmos of Judaism? In *St Mark* it is recorded that he said that the destiny of the Son of Man was to be "a ransom for many". Was that Jesus quoting Isaiah and claiming the words for himself, or Mark using Isaiah as a proof text for his own "Messiah" agenda? Calling Isaiah in as a witness or hermeneutic guide may illuminate but it also complicates.

Commentators who are instinctively sceptical about the figure of Jesus presented to us in the New Testament will want to offer a minimal account of his conscious Messianic self-identification, or any claim to Divinity; the line between those awarenesses is difficult to draw. Thomas Nagel famously asked the penetrating question, "What is it *like* to be a bat?" And answered, "We cannot possibly know." What was it like to be Jesus of Nazareth? Did he think he was divine? Probably not. Did he think he had a Divine Calling? Yes, probably.

Some madmen are convinced they are Jesus. We, who are "sane", really don't know what such a crazy conviction is like. Theresa May was convinced at the age of 22 that she was going to be Prime Minister. That turned out to be a quite rational conviction; we can understand what it is like. But we cannot know what it is like to be convinced that I am the "Son of God" with a national, possibly cosmic, destiny. Napoleon Bonaparte seems to have had a similar quite rational but less universal conviction about himself. He ended up on Elba. Some of Jesus' family and his enemies thought he might be mad, but then many of them changed their minds. He ended up on Calvary. The centurion who crucified him said (according to *Mark*) *"Truly this was [a] Son of God."* There was something about him which really was life-changing, definitely not insane. What is it like to be such a man?

The human mind is a labyrinth of tangled corridors and, whatever else he may have been, Jesus was absolutely human with a human mind like ours. We can imagine but we cannot know what it was like for him to be truly one of us *and* agent of the Cosmic Love. We have glimpses of it when "my true love has my heart and I have his". We can only speculate on the basis of our own close reading of the evidence and fill in the gaps with our own imaginative empathy, which is inevitably local, limited and partisan. Our reading of the texts is not detached. Sceptics and believers alike, we all have our own agendas, written in the ink of our own lived experience of Presence or Absence, of shifting doubts and convictions. There is a kaleidoscope of possible scenarios for each of us. But those hidden thirty years of Jesus' life formed his humanity, shaped his mind and fertilised his imagination. That is the local meat, bone and blood, and the unique life experience which constituted the humanity which was the locus of the mystery of "incarnate" Divinity. If we could know what it was really like to be such a man we might understand more solidly what Incarnation really means. And that might help us understand more clearly what saying his death was "for" us might mean. Can we take the metaphysical cloak of Divinity off his shoulders and still believe in the Incarnation? I think we can, because we know what love is like in some of its kaleidoscopic forms.

It has been said that any modern commentator or enquirer looking down the well of history will only see at the bottom of the well his own features reflected in the water. What I have written is just one such exercise in speculative imagination, written at one moment by one reader of the texts. The same hand might write a different response on another day or in other company or in a different place. I am acutely aware that in the bottom of this particular well I am seeing my own face. But it seems possible that such an exercise might ask questions, if not providing answers, suggest affirmations which can be rebutted, or lacunae which need to be filled in with other considerations.

So, what was it *like* for Jesus? A speculative "novella" by a 21st-century white, Anglo-Saxon male in his ninth decade is all I can offer. I can have very little intuitive empathy with the life of an Inuit woman in the 21st Century. What I have imagined will be even further away from the reality of a Jew's life lived in the 1st century in Palestine, but one which I do believe reveals the human face of God. That too may be a distant reflection of my own face, which is what I see when I look down a well.